StoneSoup

*The magazine supporting
creative kids around the world*

Editor
Emma Wood

Director
William Rubel

Operations
Jane Levi

Education & Production
Sarah Ainsworth

Design
Joe Ewart

D1489737

It's spring! The season of blooming flowers,
blue skies, and baby birds cheeping in their
nests. So, in this issue, in honor of spring,
I wanted to celebrate the visual in all of its
mediums. In addition to the romantic Parisian
painting, with its dreamy golds, pinks,
and blues, that graces our cover, this issue
features: a painting with a paper boat literally
pulling the piece into three dimensions; a
painted figurine that includes an ancient
Chinese poem about spring; a portfolio of
stylistically bold, bright landscapes; and
a traditional paper collage with a dark
twist. The quality and variety of the art
submissions we receive and publish in *Stone
Soup* never ceases to amaze me; I hope you
will leave this issue inspired not only by the
writing but by the visual art—in all of its
forms.

Enjoy the April showers!

Letters: We love to hear from our readers.
Please post a comment on our website or write
to us via Submittable or editor@stonesoup.
com. Your letter might be published on our
occasional Letters to the Editor page.

Submissions: Our guidelines are on the Submit
page at Stonesoup.com, where you will also find
a link to our Submittable online submissions
portal.

Subscriptions: To subscribe to *Stone Soup*,
please press the Subscribe button on our web
page, Stonesoup.com.

On the cover:
"Eiffel Tower"

**by Divya Narne, 12
Overland Park, KS**

StoneSoup
Contents

A Hardship, *mixed media*

by Alice Guo, 12
Austin, TX

A Trip to Paris?

by Claire Rinterknecht, 13
Strasbourg, France

Matthew, a travel writer with a dark past, prepares for his next trip

I visited the Shugakuin Imperial Villa on the last day of my trip. The garden is situated in the hills of the eastern suburbs of Kyoto.

Tangerine, magenta, and gold maple leaves glided down and settled on calm water like peaceful raindrops. The smudged greens and oranges of the foliage and the shadow of the rounded stone bridge merged on the pond to create a rainbow. The harmonic gong of a bell brought my gaze to a little scarlet and white pagoda. Its up-turned roof corners and nine-tiered tower made it easily recognizable. For Buddhists, each tier on the pagoda's tower represents one of nine levels of heaven. The scent of pond weed and lilies drifted up on the damp breeze. Camera snaps and elevated tourist chatter reminded me that I did not belong there. Box shrubs clustered around the edge of the pebble path. Behind them were the famous Japanese cherry blossom trees. And, every once in a while, bonsai also twisted and curled. Bonsai symbolize harmony and balance. They are grown with purposeful imperfection and the asymmetrical triangle used for their design symbolizes a continuation of life.

Japan was definitely worth the trip. It was a little frightening at first to walk around in Kyoto, so I suggest you use the subways until you get the hang of the streets. I found the Japanese were varied in their reception of an English tourist. Some grinned hugely at my accent and were willing to try to understand me, but some got annoyed at my lack of vocabulary and avoided me. Nevertheless, I wholeheartedly encourage you to plan a trip to Japan and to make sure you have the Shugakuin Imperial Villa at the top of your 'to do' list!

Matthew set down his quill and stared at his ink-stained fingers. He thought about how Blossom would have loved the Imperial Villa. Shaking his head as if to rid himself of the thought, he placed the leaves of cream paper in a brown envelope and wrote:

Travel column: Japan
by Matthew Stevens
For: The Daily Telegraph

He plucked his hat off its hook and shrugged on his green corduroy coat. His scuffed, battered briefcase in one hand, and the rattling doorknob in the other, he let himself out of the flat.

The sidewalk was cool in the early evening. Birds were singing and families were strolling home from a day at the park. *Bird song is the best kind of music in the world*, thought Matthew. Tired mothers pushed buggies with exhausted babies who drifted off to the rhythmic bumping. It had been a gorgeous day. The sun had been dazzling, the air heavy with blossoms and bird chatter. But now that evening had come, coolness rushed back in, as if trying to chase people off.

When Matthew reached the *Daily Telegraph* office, he took off his hat and stepped inside.

"Hello, Leslie." Matthew smiled at the secretary who was hunched over some papers at her desk in the foyer.

"Hello, Mr. Stevens." Leslie smiled and straightened up. "We were worried about you when we heard about the earthquake in Japan. I hope you were alright," Leslie asked with concern on her normally bright face.

"Oh yes . . . I was alright . . ." Matthew hesitated. *How had she heard about the earthquake?* "The epicenter was in the northern part of the island. Is Jane in her office?"

Leslie waited a second as if for more information, then said, "Yes, Jane is in."

Matthew thanked her and strode along the short hallway until he came to an open door with a little plaque on it reading: Jane Cunningham, Secretary and Typist. Matthew knocked lightly. Jane glanced up from her work and beckoned him inside.

"I'll be with you in a second, sir." Jane finished typing a sentence and then greeted Matthew: "Hello, Mr. Stevens."

Matthew said hello and handed her the brown envelope.

"I'll type it up straight away and get it to Mrs. Smith for tomorrow's edition. How was Japan?"

"Wonderful," Matthew replied without further explanation.

"It must have been amazing!" Jane prompted, but when she didn't get any details, she moved on. "Mrs. Smith is out at the moment, but she left a message. You're to go to France next. It has been a long time. Four years, wasn't it? Such a beautiful and romantic place," Jane ended dreamily, her eyes a little out of focus.

"Yes, France is a popular holiday destination. I like going there myself. I'll see you when I get back," Matthew answered quickly.

"Make sure you come back with a lovely story to tell."

Back outside, Matthew adjusted his briefcase and started down the narrow alleyway next to the office. At the end of the alleyway, he turned right onto a quaint street with trees lining the sidewalks and tulips in every garden; their petals faded in the twilight. At number 29, he took the steps up to a burgundy door two at a time. He hoped dinner would be ready. He rapped four times and then went to the kitchen window and tapped. A woman with his green eyes and brown hair glanced up at him and grinned, her eyes crinkling. She left the counter, leaving a man in the kitchen, and after a few seconds the front door opened.

"Matthew! You're a bit late!" She laughed.

"I know, sorry. I had to stop by the office."

They hugged, and Matthew followed her inside and placed his briefcase by the shoe rack. He took a deep breath in of spicy coconut coming from the kitchen.

"How are you, Gabrielle?"

"I'm well. And you?"

"Very well, but starving. Are you cooking curry?"

"Arthur's making his famous spicy masala."

They walked into the kitchen, but before Matthew could say hello to his brother-in-law, a flash of long flowing black hair, blue eyes, and small arms flew into his embrace.

"Matthew!!!"

Matthew hoisted the girl onto his lap as he sat down on a kitchen chair.

"Hello, Nancie. Has Robinson Crusoe satisfied your hunger for adventure?"

"Of course it hasn't! I want to go traveling with you, uncle! Where are you going next?"

"Mrs. Smith wants me to go to France. It's a holiday favorite and people want to know all about it all the time," Matthew explained.

"Can't I go with you?" Nancie didn't look at her mother because she already knew the answer. She always said no, and she knew Matthew would probably say no as well because she could barely remember the last trip they had been on together but she continued to ask him every time he came over anyway.

"Sorry, Nance, I can't take you. Anyway your mother wouldn't let you," Matthew said genially, but his gaze didn't quite reach her eyes. He looked over her head and suggested they set the table.

Matthew chased Nancie round in circles until the last spoon was laid and then they both flopped down on the red rug, exhausted from running and giggling. They lay there, laughing their heads off, until Arthur and Gabrielle came in with the masala and salad, and then they leapt up to their places at the table.

Dinner was an energetic meal. Nancie kept up a constant flow of conversation, gabbing about nothing and making up terrible jokes that she would laugh at hysterically, making everyone else laugh, so that they could share her joy.

After the dishes were washed, Matthew and Nancie went to Nancie's room where he read to her from *Alice's Adventures in Wonderland*, the new book he had brought. At one point, when Alice was walking through the woods and she saw the Cheshire cat, Matthew stopped reading.

"That reminds me of when Blossom and I went to Colorado. Blossom tried to climb a tree to see if the peak of the mountain would seem any closer, but when she came back down she said it didn't make a difference." Matthew chuckled at the memory but his voice died away quickly.

"Do you miss Blossom?" Nancie asked. "I do. I wish she were still here to show me the fun rocks to climb."

Matthew put down the book, and Nancie snuggled next to him.

"I miss Blossom very much, Nance," he said. "I miss her more than I thought was possible to miss anyone in the world."

"I miss her more than I thought was possible to miss anyone in the world."

Matthew unlocked the door to his quiet apartment and flicked on the light bulb. He hung up his coat and hat and on his way down the corridor placed his briefcase on a wooden chest full of books.

Matthew put water on the stove to boil and watched its still surface slowly agitate with tiny bubbles coming up from the bottom of the pan. It was funny, Matthew thought, how they came up in such perfectly straight lines and then disappeared when there was no more water to move through. *Like raindrops*, he thought, *going in the opposite direction.*

Matthew found the teapot, put in some black tea leaves, and poured the boiling water on top. While the tea was steeping, he went over to the bookshelf where all the European travel books were and ran his fingers along their spines.

"Ah-ha!" he said aloud when he found the one he wanted. He thumbed through it to make sure it had a chapter on Paris and then continued to search for other books. By the time his tea had steeped, there was a teetering pile of paperbacks about France resting on the armchair.

He settled down with his tea and books and read long into the night. He visited Paris, Strasbourg, Lyon, and many other places besides. Matthew read so long that he fell asleep in his chair.

When he awoke, he found himself as he had been the night before, apart from the fact that his empty teacup had tipped in his lap and several books had fallen to the floor. He quickly picked them up and placed them back on the chair. In the kitchen, he set his teacup on the counter and looked at the clock: 6:30. Matthew decided he might as well start the day, so he reached for a mason jar from the cupboard, took the peanut butter and soy milk from the refrigerator, a banana from the fruit bowl, and the hot chocolate powder from the shelf. He put everything in the jar and the blender whirred it all together.

As he sat at the table to drink his smoothie, he heard a knock at the door.

"Gabrielle! Nancie!" he exclaimed in surprise when he saw who it was.

"Matthew! I'm sorry to disturb you so early in the morning but I just got a call from work, and I have to go in straight away. Arthur has already gone so I was wondering if you could look after Nancie for a few hours?"

"Yes, of course. Have you had breakfast yet, Nancie?"

"No." Nancie yawned and leaned against her mother.

"I was just about to have mine, so you can join me," Matthew took her hand. "Go on, Gabrielle, or you'll be late for work."

"Thank you, Matthew! I'll pick her up at lunchtime or I'll call," she shouted back as she rushed down the hallway.

"Come on, Nance. It looks like you

got out of bed a little too early this morning," Matthew chuckled.

Nancie yawned again in reply.

Matthew led her into the living room. He hastily moved all the books off of the armchair and onto the coffee table so Nancie could curl up in it. Next, he set about cooking a hot breakfast. He baked apple muffins and fried eggs (he didn't like scrambled eggs and neither did Nancie) and then blended up Nancie's favorite frozen berry and yogurt smoothie. The warm smells of Matthew's cooking drifted over to Nancie, and she roused slowly and rubbed her eyes of sleep.

"Matthew, why do you have all these books about France out? You're about to be there; you don't need to read about it!" she proclaimed.

"It never hurts to know more about where you're going. Anyway, most of these are travel guides." Matthew turned back to the counter, away from Nancie.

Nancie held up one of the books. "This one isn't. Look, *The Hunchback of Notre-Dame*, and this one isn't either . . . or this one." Nancie held up several books.

"Oh? I must have put the guides in my room then," Matthew quickly busied himself by cracking eggs into a hot pan.

"Matthew?"

"Yes, Nance?"

"What kind of adventure do you think you'll have in France?"

Matthew smiled and finished salting the eggs. He loved it when Nancie asked him that question.

"Well now. I'll sit by the Seine while drinking a glass of Bordeaux and eating Camembert on freshly baked baguette. I'll watch the sun turn the water to liquid gold and set the trees on fire. Fairy lights will twinkle in the dying light and the romantic hush of French voices will drift along with the current of the Seine. Butterflies will land next to me and tiny forget-me-nots will nod their heads. Aubrieta and black-eyed Susans clustered at the base of the bridge will sway in time to the allegretto played on a piano by delicate fingers."

"Is that what France is really like?" Nancie said, amazed.

"Yes." Matthew placed a hot plate in front of Nancie, then sat down with his own breakfast.

"It sounds splendid. I wish I could come. Are you sure—"

"Quite sure. I will take you to the park, though, if you finish up your breakfast."

"But I . . . alright," Nancie sighed and finished her smoothie.

Before they left, Matthew made sure he had his briefcase, a pad of paper, and a pen. He made Nancie wear a sweater, put on his own coat and hat, and then they walked out the door.

The park was relatively large with a playground at the center. Buttercups and tulips covered the bright lawn. It was still chilly outside, but Matthew could tell it would be another lovely day. The only sounds were their voices and those of the birds. When they got to the playground, Nancie went straight to the climbing structure. Matthew wasn't surprised; he knew how much Nancie liked to climb. He sat on a bench near the bottom of the structure and set his briefcase beside him. He took the pad of paper from under his arm and began writing. Every once in a while, he would look up at Nancie to make sure she was alright. He got nervous when she climbed, and he didn't like to take his eyes off her for more than a few minutes at a time. As Nancie was nearing the top, Matthew had an idea spark and was scribbling quickly when he heard the scream. His eyes flashed up and he jumped to his feet. He saw Nancie lose her grip and tip backwards. His blood went cold. *Nancie!* His long strides got him to the structure just as she fell. Matthew caught her in his arms and put her down gently. His arms were shaking badly.

"Are you okay? Are you hurt?" Matthew inquired with a trembling voice.

"I'm okay. I just got scared."

"Never do that again, Nance, alright? You nearly killed me." Matthew sat down next to her.

"Sorry, Matthew." She hugged him, and he held her tightly. That's when he noticed his papers. In his haste to catch Nancie, Matthew had let all the papers fly out of his lap, and they were now strewn all over the ground. Nancie and Matthew went over and started to pick them up. Matthew moved as quickly as possible and whenever Nancie picked one up he took it from her as soon as she had it in her hands. But Nancie saw snatches of his writing, however hard Matthew tried to hide it from her. She picked up the last one and then stepped back so Matthew couldn't take it. She read the first few lines.

"Thank you, Nancie." Matthew reached out his arm demonstrating that she needed to hand him the paper. "Go play while I finish tidying this up."

But Nancie didn't move. She stayed as still as a statue.

"Go on, Nancie, just don't play on the climbing structure anymore," Matthew insisted.

Nancie still didn't budge and didn't hand back the paper she clutched in one hand.

She began to read off the sheet: "The sun was falling behind the trees, catching them on fire. As it touched the earth with its magnificence, the Seine turned to liquid gold and a soft allegretto started up somewhere high above, played by delicate fingers. Butterflies twirled in the air, dancing to the music. Clustered at the base of the bridge, tiny forget-me-nots nodded their heads and dandelions shook their manes."

She stared up at Matthew in confusion. "This is the story that you told me this morning. Why are you writing the column when you haven't been to France yet?"

"Nancie, come here." Matthew gestured for her to sit next to him on the bench.

Nancie joined him. Matthew took

As Nancie was nearing the top, Matthew had an idea spark and was scribbling quickly when he heard the scream.

a deep breath, lifted his briefcase onto his lap, and undid the clasp. Matthew's hands shook as he took out two passports and a few photographs.

"These are the photos from my last trip. And our passports. Blossom's and mine. This was the last photo I took of her before she died." Matthew held up the crinkled photo of a woman in shorts and an orange t-shirt. "She was laughing because I had just told her a joke. She let go of the boulder she was climbing and fell. I couldn't catch her. She was too far away. She shouldn't have died. I ran to help, but I wasn't quick enough. I haven't gone anywhere since. I'm too afraid that something else might happen." He fumbled with one of the passports. The portrait of a slender woman with round amber eyes and chestnut hair gazed up at them.

"She never liked having her photo taken for her passport because she couldn't smile. She said that if she couldn't smile she wasn't who she was," Matthew said in a hushed voice.

Nancie gently took the photos that Matthew had set aside and stared at the top one. It was of the same woman, but this time her eyes were laughing and Matthew was with her. They were standing on a bridge, the water behind them a dull blue because the sky was overcast. The dismal weather had not dampened the young lovers' spirits. They both beamed at the camera. The next photo was of Blossom again, where she sat in front of the Eiffel Tower, the sun kissing her face. The last one was of Blossom with her arms outstretched and her head tilted back as she looked up at the sky and let the rain drench her from head to toe.

"Matthew? Why did you pretend to keep traveling? Why didn't you just stop and tell everyone?"

"I'm not sure, Nance. I suppose I thought that if I continued to write the column, I could pretend that I was getting over Blossom. I also didn't want to disappoint you and was embarrassed that I was scared. Also, I needed the money. How would I pay my bills?"

"You could have come to live at our house," Nancie said.

Matthew hugged Nancie. He didn't know what he would do without her. He held her tight, thankful that she didn't let go. He was still her idol, even if he made gigantic mistakes.

The sky had greyed, and a brisk wind made Matthew pull his corduroy coat around Nancie. The air rumbled with a passing airplane.

"Take me with you to Paris," Nancie said.

Matthew considered his courageous niece and smiled.

Then he stood up and held out his hand, and together they walked with renewed purpose out of the park. In Matthew's free hand, he held his briefcase, considerably lighter than it had been the day before. He was ready to go on a new adventure.

Chinese Calabash Girls

by Ziqing Peng, 10
Nanjing, China

Chinese Calabash I, *Chinese ink, watercolors, and calabash*

Chinese Calabash II, *Chinese ink, watercolors, and calabash*

On my second calabash, I drew a Chinese poem written by Wang Anshi, a famous prime minister of the Northern Song Dynasty. The poem describes the Spring Festival in ancient China. Here is the poem in Chinese and its translation in English.

Spring Festival Eve
by Wang Anshi (1021-1086)
Written during the Northern Song Dynasty (960-1127)

元日
(北宋) 王安石
爆竹声中一除,
春风送暖入屠苏。
千门万户瞳瞳日,
总把新桃旧符。

Firecrackers are shouting goodbye to the last year,
In warm spring breeze people drink tusu wine.
Thousands of households greet the bright rising sun,
Replacing each couplet on the door with a new one.

Joyous Ensemble

by Sabrina Guo, 12
Oyster Bay, NY

A violinist on tour in China contemplates the power of music

In Shenzhen, China, the night before my first performance on tour with the Joyous String Ensemble, one of the youngest string ensembles in the world, I dreamt of a plum. Up close, it was a combination of pink, red, and orange. In front of me, two paths intersected, forming a shape like a cross, with an aqua pond in the middle and a spectacular fountain hovering in midair that had flowing, agile water, spouting melted diamonds and crystals. I looked down and was surprised to see that I was floating above the glass path, which encased running water with huge koi and calypso fish. They swam smoothly and gracefully, whipping their tails in an airy, wavelike way. There were a bunch of trees surrounding me. I could smell fruity scents and the cherry blossoms; the aroma was pure and sweet, not at all strong and overwhelming like most garden scents. I tried propelling myself by swinging my arms like helicopter blades. I went *up . . . up . . .* and *up . . .* as if I might touch the clouds.

The next night, I felt a bright white light on me. Then green. Then blue. Then purple, which made the violin look orange and made my Pirastro Evah Pirazzi Gold's bottom glow in the dark. The light testing was over. I smiled at the audience and waved, following the others, and tried my best to look straight ahead, not at anyone in particular. There was just this blurry wavering sea of heads stretched in every direction. I raised my violin to my chin, and we began our set.

Accompanying us on the piano was Mr. Julian Yu, the director of the Joyous String Ensemble and an accomplished composer, conductor, and performing pianist. He has been an inspirational mentor, teaching us how to genuinely enjoy the wonders of music. He said that music is not just a sound but also an emotion, like happiness, sadness, regret, or love. He's encouraged us to use the power of music to spread love and kindness. He believes that music can help save lives and change the world. I doubted this at first, but now, I believe that all of these ideas are within reach.

As I played that night, I was brimming with nervousness, but I focused on how happy everyone had looked on the car ride to the theater. My happiest memories of being in this ensemble have taken place right before each performance—everyone excited and ready to communicate with the audience through music. Our first piece was "Summer" by Vivaldi, which slowly morphed into "Smooth Criminal" by Michael Jackson. Adrenaline flooded my body; the energy around the stage was magnetic, and I felt my bow moving with forces that seemed inside and outside of me at the same time. I smiled in my heart and wondered if my friends felt the same. The first set flew by, and then the second, and before I knew it the performance was over! So quickly, it was hard to track individual moments, but by the end, standing up before an audience cheering and hooting—my crazy dad especially, who kept yelling through his cupped hands—suggested it had been a success. I just kept thinking to myself, *keep smiling* . . .

After the performance, we rode back to our hotel, where we were staying high up on the 24th floor. I gazed out the window to the streets busy with people scrambling about, advertising salesmen shoving papers into people's hands, bicycles zigzagging in every direction. My parents called to me, reminding me to get my rest, since the next day we'd be leaving early for Beijing. I flopped into bed, cactus-style, and couldn't help smiling again, replaying parts of the performance before I fell asleep.

I had yellow watermelon for breakfast the next morning. It was soft, not as crisp as the red kind I was used to, but sweeter. It took me a while to wrap my brain around yellow juice and black seeds meshed together. Yet another reminder that I was in a new place, far from home, where I couldn't expect to follow the same routine, or to experience the same tastes, smells, or sounds. Same as the music of chopsticks clinking together like a drum beat, the sound of knobs turning to send hotpots clicking, the flicker of flames erupting under dishes. Around the corner from our hotel, there was a small alleyway with a bunch of restaurants and a bakery. The next morning, when we left to catch our ride, the whole street was alive with spices filling my nose, sweetly offset by freshly baked bread and sugar.

Our second performance was even more nerve-wracking because we would be performing with Master Lu Si Qing, the best violinist in China and one of my idols. The fact that I was going to accompany him seemed impossible. When we first met him backstage, I marveled over his shiny blue jacket and perfectly creased pants. On stage, he stood before us, chasing the melody of every piece. I felt his raw energy as he rocked and swayed, almost like the violin was an extension of his body, the music living inside him all along. Almost every face in the audience hid behind a videotaping phone, which I imagined made us look like little halos of light around our master. We accompanied him for Vivaldi's Double Concerto, another dizzying blur. I remember this intense feeling of fatigue and excitement afterward, as the audience roared in a standing ovation. Each young player received a rose, and I was thrilled to get the reddish purple one I'd been hoping for, one that reminded me of the plum in my dream. We all exited the stage, and I was surprised when we were served glasses of water on a black tray. I slowly sipped the water, relishing its smooth, sweet taste.

That night, my memory traveled back to my family's earlier visit to Shenzhen. We had visited an antique store, where there were glass displays with little sky-blue vases with clover-like plants that only had one leaf: two thin stalks in each vase. In the corner, there was a long table from ancient times with a large wooden turtle sitting on it. My parents used to tell me these animals are symbols of wisdom, and I think that's true because they live for a long time and move so slowly, like they've seen it all and don't understand any hurry. I walked over to the table with my father, who told me how to check if it was authentically as old as it appeared. You look for stripped logs placed horizontally on top, with wooden planks below for support. After we examined it, we could tell it was truly an ancient table. In the U.S., we seem to value the physical appearance of things over their history or the traditions and stories implied by them. I started to think every object was part of a story or larger dream that can come alive through travel and music.

At the Shanghai concert, we were surrounded by people everywhere. We were on an enormous platform, and there was the audience—behind us, next to us, in front of us, and above us. Not only was this the biggest show yet, but this time we were raising money through ticket sales and autograph signings for a 14-year-old boy's mother who needed a lifesaving surgery. The boy was a talented singer, but since China doesn't have many performance events for his age group, he lacked the opportunity to raise the money for his mother alone. The leader of our group is Justin Yu, the 11-year-old son of our director, who is already a world-famous cellist. The boy came out to sing with him for one of the numbers. It was a very emotional moment, feeling the boy's spirit there on the stage, and afterward, I watched some people in the audience wipe their eyes through a thunder of applause. It was the first time that I had ever performed with a higher purpose in mind, beyond wanting to share my love of music with the world, for a family in need. The tour ended, and we received a letter from the boy's father with news that the surgery had worked. While Mr. Yu had told us that music could help to save lives, I hadn't quite believed him until I read that letter. We all felt so moved and honored to be part of that success.

Later that night, I had another dream. Time was frozen, and there were a bunch of string instruments floating around, moving one millimeter per second. I plucked the A-string of a violin in midair, which created a big wave of echoes that blasted my eardrums. The strange thing was,

I could see the sound waves. The A-string made a strawberry-colored wave, D made a yellow wave, while G was sienna, and E was green. Each instrument produced different colored waves, as if they were part of a realm behind the music. Sometimes I wonder if my dreams are synesthesiac, with sounds forming colors through my memory. All the music swirled around my brain at night and pranced around like horses. I wondered if this was all part of living the music, not just practicing and playing it, but feeling its forces upon me, like a liquid that had begun to pump through my heart and lungs, sustaining me through these weeks. Somehow, I played three more concerts with the same energy as the first, and time only seemed to speed up with each—this continual flow of motion that I became more accustomed to, making it harder to separate out individual memories afterward.

I have visited China many times before. Ever since I was three, I've been traveling with my parents to Shenyang to visit my extended family. Usually, we stay at my aunt's house, where they have a fish tank and a little bonsai tree I like to watch my aunt trim. I also like the feel of the tiny leaves, sharp like needles. They always make me think of a miniature world that exists beyond my imagination. Invisible birds and rivers making inaudible sounds. Some mornings, if we wake early enough, we walk to the morning market, where we shop for everything from fried pure milk to jewelry and barbecued squid. Nearby, there is also a sushi restaurant with fresh octopus and salmon rolls. We always eat in the room where the floor makes noises like tapping ice. Above, there is a chandelier: like glass stars suspended in the air, dangling from a thin hook, encrusted in a zodiac of birthstones. The breeze from the AC causes them to swing from side to side as if they were flowers swaying to a forgotten melody.

These memories transport me back to the moment I am living now, in the wake of last summer's China tour. Sometimes I feel music is a special language of memory between times and places. Music reminds me of an open door to a clear sky. Sometimes, I feel what you want to say can be conveyed better in music than in words. Music carries my feelings, the same way memories do, one thing leading to the next and the next, all through shared emotions between people, placing those people within reach of one another. Sometimes I think memory and music work together like a dream: I start remembering one place and all of its images seep out in a colorful spiral of smells and tastes and sounds, all capturing the soul of a place, a period of time. And then I wake up from that dream and wonder how I got from there to here and back again, as if my memory is one continuous map, this circle of song printed inside me.

Gilmanton at Night

by Anya Geist, 12
Worcester, MA

The crickets chirp, sing to the starry night.

The floorboards creak and moan of old age.

The wallpaper stands rigid, but cracked and peeling.

The motorcycles rev and talk back and forth by the road.

The two old Volvos settle in on the grassy lot.

A musty, old-yet-comforting smell seeps everywhere in the house.

I turn over in bed, to look at moonlight streaming through the gaping crack in the
shade.

Across the street, the antique store is boarded up,

Its precious relics waiting until tomorrow.

The corner store is closed, sodas and water closed up,

Coffee makers quiet, until the morning brew.

Down at the pond, the bathhouse looms quietly, old green paint on the outside.

Swimsuits and towels hang on racks in rooms, swaying in a soft breeze.

The day's sand tracked in is leaking through the old planks on the floor,

Falling onto the ground beneath.

The raft bobs in the pond, surrounded by dark glistening water.

Up the dirt road to Drew Farm,

Wild animals roam the backyard.

In the attic, the lights are off.

In the room at the back, mattresses, chairs, tables, and papers are left sprawled out

In the middle of planning.

In Airy Cottage, the lights are out,

The radio, always playing orchestras, is off and quiet.

Back in the Little House, all the screen doors are locked

And the porch furniture stands still on the porch.

This is Gilmanton at night.

The House

The cicadas chirp a lullaby to the night.

Their buzzing seems obtrusive at first

But grows to be comforting and content.

Inside, the tiled floor sits cold with all its rivets and dips.

Shutters are locked shut to the windows,

Hatches battened down,

Giving the impression of the quarters of a ship

Sailing through the long, dry grasses of Southern France.

In the beige bedroom, I lie on the twin bed, my shoulder leaning against the wall.

My friend lies across the room, snoring peacefully.

Outside, down the hallway, the fifth bedroom lays vacant.

The other three are occupied, their doors shut tightly.

The steep, tiled stairs lead the way down to the first floor,

Its high ceiling grand but inviting.

The two L-shaped couches in the back living room host card boxes

From games previously played.

These floors are new and wooden.

The windows there still show outside, onto the small cracked patio.

The kitchen is on the front left side of the house,

Cramped but piled with food

And giving way to the laundry room with its low, stooped ceiling.

The dining room table is cleared off,

Its blue tablecloth lit up by the moon that shines bright through the windows.

The alcoves in it are in shadow, mysterious and dark.

The great front door creaks on its old hinges.

Breezes whish through the air,

Spreading the smell of overripe fruit from the trees.

The cars and table sit on a rough gravel.

Through a grove, the pool sits dark.

Its sloshing can be heard, a welcoming sound.

Five chairs sit under an umbrella, relaxing.

A yard of dry grasses stretches until a set of bushes.

From the yard, the whole city seems to be seen.

All of the narrow streets and alleys and squares of Aix-en-Provence.

The mountain of Sainte-Victoire looms in the distance,

Standing where it can just be seen.

Returning through the small grove, the house is sleepy and tired.

The shutters are closed and the windows on the first floor are empty and dark

Even as the moon shines on the front of the house.

The old, worn stone is cool to the touch in the dry night.

Back in bed, I lay under the blanket, chilly

And think of the house perched on its hill

Sleeping under the canopy of night.

Portfolio

by John P. Anson, 7
Kerala, India

The Sky at Night and Day, *oil pastels*

Beautiful Forest, *oil pastels*

Train that Going Through a Forest, *oil pastels*

Eternal Friendship

by Blanche Li, 9
Danville, CA

A girl struggles to overcome an old fear in order to accept a new friend

My mom and I walked through the narrow hallway, noticing all the people around us. I saw a girl in a purple floral dress standing next to her dad. She looked a little younger than I was. I wondered if we were going to be friends. After that, I saw a cast on the girl's right arm, a type of cast I had never seen before. It looked like decorated plastic. Quickly, I glanced away because I knew it was rude to stare. Still, what was that? It didn't look like a cast. I thought it was unusual. Absent-mindedly, I strolled the rest of the way to the classroom.

When we were finally inside, I saw that four students were sitting in their chairs and were unpacking their cellos in a great rush, as if they were police searching bags. One of the students even chipped his cello because he was in such a hurry to be the first to unpack and get the best seat. I looked up at the ceiling. It looked kind of like those dance ceilings full of beams. I guessed they were used for supporting the floors above it.

Just then, I noticed that the girl I had previously seen was taking off her arm! I was blank for a minute. Then I knew it. Her right arm was actually artificial. Next, she took something out of a large grocery bag. It seemed like an advanced bionic arm. It was tan and white. Its shape made me feel as if the arm were twisted all around. I could see the technology at work. She handed the bionic arm to her dad, who was a tall and silent man. His attention was focused only on his daughter. He twisted it a few times on her arm and then "Click!"—it was on.

During the group lesson, I learned from our teacher that the girl's name was Kylie. Kylie's bionic arm had two clips. One was fastened to a modified bridge that supported the strings of her cello and one was fastened to her bionic arm. This way, when Kylie played, the bow wouldn't slide off the cello. Her dad also put a Bow-Right on the bridge, a two-piece metal frame that was fastened to both sides of the bridge. It was looped by rubber bands and many small pieces of cushion. I pondered why Kylie needed so many cushions on her cello. Finally, I understood that this way, the cello would not get chipped or scratched.

I started wondering if I should pay attention to Kylie and be friends with her. Sometimes I have nightmares about people with disabilities. Once I met a boy who had lost two of his fingers. I didn't know if I was going to have a nightmare about Kylie. Maybe not. I wasn't sure at all. Sometimes, all these nightmares start to pop into my head. I didn't know if I was going to have terrifying dreams about her. I thought she might scare me off in my dream. But I was still hesitating. The only problem was I still wanted a friend.

Kylie was still sitting next to me. When she was playing, I noticed something else. Her other hand's fingers were half the length of my own. That brightened my heart up. She made me feel like she was amazing and talented. I couldn't believe she could play the cello.

When Kylie left early that day because she was tired, a girl in the class asked, "What happened to her?"

My teacher just replied, "She was born like that." I wasn't sure if my teacher really meant it. Maybe it was just a secret that Kylie, her family, and her teacher shared.

One month later, my teacher set up a free 30-minute play-together for Kylie and me. We got to play duets, holiday songs, and games with each other. It was really fun. I realized that Kylie was a great, energetic girl. She asked questions, said "hi" to everyone she saw, and was never afraid to make mistakes. Gradually, Kylie and I became friends. Slowly, my fear of nightmares about Kylie disappeared. I learned that the nightmares come to me only if I let them. If I think about them too much, the nightmares overtake my brain. It is kind of like they are gum stuck to the corner of my mind. Once they are there, I can't get them off. They only loosen when I'm sleeping, and then the devastating dreams about snakes and ghosts happen. If I don't let them come into my head, they won't come. And in each of my schools I have been to, I remember at least one of my friends who had a disability. I now knew that disabilities were normal. All my friends who had disabilities could be the same as me. They could eat ice cream, they could play games and instruments, and they could always have smiles on their faces.

Then one day, news from my teacher overloaded my brain. Kylie was coming to a six-day cello camp with me in Washington! I wanted to jump up and down and laugh with joy! I could not believe it. How would she play in front of a crowd without being frightened? If I were her, I would be terrified that I would make a mistake, and I would be scared that people would look at me as if I were someone to gawk at. I could imagine this because there was once a boy at my old school named Josh who always called me "lima bean girl" when I had a scar on my face. And guess what? After a few minutes, all my friends came to call me that. No one likes that kind of attention.

I learned that the nightmares come to me only if I let them

I waited and waited for the day to come. The day I would be able to talk to Kylie and have fun again. Finally, it came.

The day I met Kylie at cello camp was a cool day with the sun shining its bright rays over us. I was really excited to talk to her.

The lessons were 12 hours long. We had to stay with each other all the time. At first, I thought fear would return to my brain. But I knew that it was just a silly thing for a girl like me to think of.

Our teachers grouped Kylie and me into a pair. We shared music stands. Kylie helped me find which building to go to. Once we got there, I quickly unpacked and helped set up our benches and stands. Kylie had a great memory. She remembered the right music piece we needed for our lesson. On the last day of camp, we had a recital. Our music was several pages long. While playing, our right hands were occupied by the bow so we had to use our left hands to quickly turn the page. When I turned the page, it was very likely that the rest of the music on the stand would drop. When it was time to flip the pages, Kylie held the other side of the music on the stand. This way, we could move onto the next music seamlessly. After the recital, Kylie and I gave each other a Bow-Five. We had collaborated so well. Even our camp teachers couldn't help noticing it.

Kylie told me that she has two bionic arms. One has a stripe pattern and one has a rainbow print. She also told me that her bionic arm grows with her. One afternoon, during the lesson break, I held one of her bionic arms and gazed at it in wonder. Kylie looked at me. Without a word, she reached out her hand and touched my face. I turned my eyes to her. I could feel her friendship orbiting my body. It was a gentle, friendly, and warm feeling. It felt like everlasting friendship.

To my parents, I am a wonder. To Kylie's parents, she is a wonder. Making new friends is also a wonder. There are lots of wonders in the world. Open your hand, grab them, and they will be within your reach.

The Juggle Man

by Annalise Braddock, 7
Katonah, NY

One day I went to the juggle place and on a shelf sat the juggle man.

He said to me you took a juggle now give it back to me.

The owner of the juggle place said to go home and then she called the police.

The police said outside there is young poor Sally with balls in hand but cannot juggle.

Then the police said on a Monday you took a suitcase on Tuesday you took a toothbrush and on Friday you poured milk.

What a bad girl you have been.

Color City, *paper collage*

by Adhi Sukhdial, 7
Stillwater, OK

Honor Roll

Welcome to the *Stone Soup* Honor Roll. Every month we receive submissions from hundreds of kids from around the world. Unfortunately, we don't have space to publish all the great work we receive. We want to commend some of these talented writers and artists and encourage them to keep creating.

Fiction
Annie Baker-Young, 8
Ava Horton, 13
Aaron Huang, 12
Marilena Korahais, 8
Liliana McCowan, 11
Selina Ni, 11
Pip Reese, 8
Sarah Zimmerman, 12

Poetry
Talia Chin, 7
Amity Doyle, 9
Yaelin Hough, 12
Celia Miller Pitt, 12
Kathleen Werth, 9
Sasha Yelagina, 9

Art
Sarah Berry, 13
Story Kummer, 12

Visit the *Stone Soup* store at Stonesoupstore.com to buy:

- Magazines—individual issues of *Stone Soup*, past and present.
- Books—our collection of themed anthologies (fantasy, sport, poetry, and more), and the *Stone Soup Annual* (all the year's issues, plus a flavor of the year online, in one volume).
- Art prints—high quality prints from our collection of children's art
- Journals and sketchbooks for writing and drawing

...and more!

Don't forget to visit Stonesoup.com to browse our bonus materials. There you will find:

- 20 years of back issues—around 5,000 stories, poems, and reviews
- Blog posts from our young bloggers on subjects from sports to sewing—plus ecology, reading, and book reviews
- Video interviews with *Stone Soup* authors
- Music, spoken word, and performances

CPSIA information can be obtained
at www.ICGtesting.com
Printed in the USA
BVHW062312040319
541783BV00002B/4/P